Gully
Gets a Take-Away
By Jon Cleave

Published in 2006
© 2006 Jonathan Cleave

www.thegullery.co.uk

ISBN-10: 0-9553165-1-0
ISBN-13: 978-0-9553165-1-7

Text and illustrations copyright © 2005 Jonathan Cleave
The rights of Jonathan Cleave to be identified as author and illustrator of this work has been
asserted by him in accordance with the Copyright, Designs and Patents Act 1988.
Design by Brad Waters www.bwgd.co.uk
Printed in the Westcountry by The Printing Press

For Caroline

you know it's not good for you...

...pie and chips and ketchup. and chicken. burger and pasty. lots of nuggets. cod. cheeseburger. salt and pepper...

Have I ever pinched your little brother's ice cream or dive bombed your granny?
Or done a great big sploshy splattt all over your dad's clean shiny car? Well
I'm so sorry, its nothing personal. Just doing my job, that's all.

Anyway, there's not much you can do about it. We're protected. By the law. Oh yes, and if you mess or fiddle with us or our chicks or our eggs or nests, or do anything else horrid that we don't like, it's just like stealing or murder. We'll squeal on you to the police and you could end up in court in front of the beak!

...his honour Judge Gully the beak presiding in court...

And guess who protected us in the first place? That's right; it was you! Now I might be a bird brain, but did you *really* mean to do that?

Loads of my mates have moved into the village to live, up on the rooftops in what we call the gullery. Well, who would want to live on a draughty cold old ledge high up on a cliff when you can have the comfort of your own nice cottage roof?

Me and the princess, that's what I call the missus, live on Mrs Baker's roof, down in a dip and next to her warm chimney, and she feeds us bits of bread and cake and scones and things. In return, I never pooh on her or on the washing on her line, and never dive bomb her to scare her half to death or keep her awake all night with my awful squawking.

No. If I want to do any of that, I go next door.

Normally, next door is empty. But for two weeks every year, there are people in there. They are not at all like Mrs Baker. They are the Trumpers from Bristol, and next door is their holiday cottage.

Mr Trumper, who is called Lionel, is not nice. He is big and fat, and has more chins than a Chinese telephone directory, and on his holidays always wears tiny, shiny, bulgy football shorts and a silly 'Fat Willy' tee shirt, with his bulbous belly bloating out from underneath it. And, worst of all, on Lionel's belly, *in* his belly, is the deepest, hairiest belly button you have ever seen, and he is always digging at it with his finger, hooking out bits of fluff, and rolling them into balls to flick at his son, Tyrone. No, Lionel is not nice.

Lionel waving...can you see
the nasty, fluffy belly button?

You should not be surprised to learn that Tyrone isn't very nice either. Tyrone spends his summer holidays throwing sticks and stones at me and the princess and the other gulls, and he steals our eggs to throw at Mrs Baker's door and then runs off laughing, and when she comes out Lionel shouts at her 'Leave the boy alone, he's only having a bit of fun, you old bag!'.

Tyrone's mum, Honeysuckle Trumper, wears huge dresses. When she walks, she is like a flowery pirate ship under full sail, with bright, splodgy begonias and petunias all billowing in the wind. It is a marvelous sight to behold. Honeysuckle smells beautifully of several sorts of perfume, and every few minutes she sprays herself with a new one that she plucks from the bottom of her bag. Lionel says that this helps to keep the flies away.

Tyrone having lots of fun on the beach

Honeysuckle looked like a flowery pirate ship under full sail!

But the most striking thing about Honeysuckle is her singing. Wherever she goes she sings at the very top of her voice. Hits of the seventies normally, although she has been known to dabble with songs from the shows, and this would be ok if her voice was not like that of a tone deaf rook with a sore throat and megaphone….

Sabre likes her singing. Sabre is the Trumper's dog. He is a monster, with a huge head and jaws and a studded leather collar around his thick neck, and he looks very fierce. But, and this is a good thing, Sabre is a big baby cowardy-custard who would run away from even the smallest, cutest kitten.

'Stupid mutt,' says Lionel. 'Why don't you get rid of it to the dog's home…or have it put down or summat?'

'He likes me singing, don't you darling?' says Honeysuckle, and Sabre just wags his stumpy tail.

And that's what me and the princess and all the other gulls have to put up with every year, the Trumpers. Now I'm a patient sort of gull who can put up with most things. But one thing I cannot stand is having my food mucked around with, and that was the Trumper's first *big* mistake.

Now we gulls don't eat scraps of stinking, rotten old fish or wiggly, wriggly worms any more, that sort of stuff is revolting and we have moved on to fast food take-away, deep fry, call it what you will. I find it so convenient, and there is so much of it about these days, so much choice. Most of the time, I have to dig around in the bins

The take-away and lots of my mates...

and ferret about a bit, and drag the crumpled fish and chip wrappers out and shake 'em to get the morsels to drop out, and for some reason it seems to annoy some people that I don't tidy the wrappers away afterwards.

Well tough. I'm protected.

However the best, most definitely the best, are fresh fried meals straight out of The Jolly Smuggler's Take-Away, and by far the greatest thing about this, something sadly missing when you are reduced to scavenging from bins or bags, is the thrill of the chase.

But I don't want you to think that Mrs Baker's cake and bread treats are left to waste, they're not. It would be ungrateful and rude not to take these, and I would never want to hurt her feelings, and so all together the princess and I have a nicely balanced diet.

Nicely balanced that is, until the Trumpers arrive.

It was one fine, sunny August day, when from up in the gullery I heard them walking home from the beach.
'Sailing, oh we're sailing, home again across the…'
'For gawd's sakes give it a rest, Honey darling! You're even drowning out that low flying jet …' scowled Lionel.
'Dad, dad! Look! Sabre's eating the cake that the old bags put out!'

'He ain't no fool, that 'un. Go on my son, fill yer boots for free. Daft old bags only left it out for them bloomin' gulls. They can starve for a change!' said Lionel.

I peered down from the roof. Sure enough, Sabre was eating the lot. To be fair, it did look delicious. Two bits of battenburg cake, all pink and yellow sponge and marzipan, a fruit scone with some strawberry jam, and a Mr Kipling fondant fancy. *And* she'd put them on a paper doily for me.

Sabre was eating the lot!

Lionel looked up and spotted me.

'Yeah!' he said. 'Go on, get lost you flying rat!'

I thought this was very unkind of him. Mrs Baker opened her door.

'Excuse me…'she said.

'Yeah, and you get lost n'all you old bag, before I sets our Sabre here on ya!'

She closed her door. Lionel laughed. Sabre whimpered. Tyrone chewed a piece of my marzipan.

'Come on,' he said. 'I'm hungry now. Lets get a take-away…'

'…*Food, glorious food, fried jelly and mustard, While we're in the mood…*' sang Honeysuckle.

Sabre wagged his stump.

'Oi! No one's in the mood for that row! Shut it and lets eat!' said Lionel.

He had no idea that I understood. How could I? I'm just a flying rat, after all.

It was time they were taught a lesson.

Take-away. Double take-away. The Trumpers take-away from the chippy, and I take-away from them. What a marvelous idea, simply marvelous. With brains like we've got, its no wonder you protected us!

I wonder what we shall be having …

I flew high up over the village and looked down on the greedy Trumpers, all loaded up with their take-aways and heading for the public benches overlooking the harbour. My shadow passed over them, but they had no idea that I was up there, and I circled around and around observing strict air silence, awaiting the perfect moment.

To get a better view of my supper, I lost altitude by maybe twenty feet. My targets, the Trumpers, were sitting all in a row on a bench, each opening their wrappers on their knees and drooling with hunger.

My shadow over the Trumpers

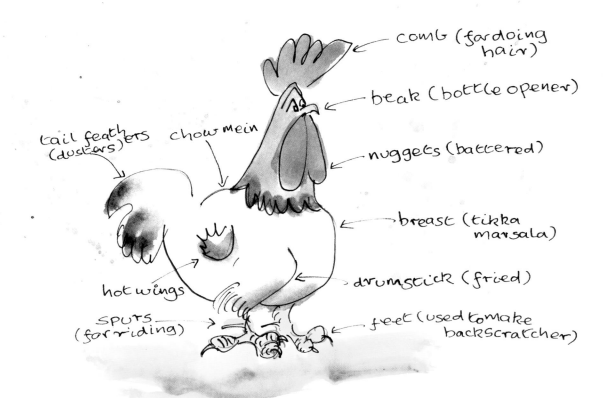

comb (for doing hair)

beak (bottle opener)

nuggets (battered)

breast (tikka marsala)

drumstick (fried)

feet (used to make backscratcher)

tail feathers (dusters)

chow mein

hot wings

spurs (for riding)

Bits of a chicken...I'm glad you don't eat us gulls!

Tyrone had chosen chicken nuggets and chips, delicious but for me impractical. You try snatching ten nuggets with one beak in one swoop…its not easy, unless you're a pelican or a juggler of course! A chicken drumstick would have been easier, perhaps a southern fried one, or even a hot chicken wing, they're nice. Anyway, the ghastly Tyrone had smeared all the nuggets in that dreadful red ketchupy stuff, which neither I or the princess like, so I decided not to try and pinch them.

But Honeysuckle, who was sitting in the middle between Tyrone and Lionel, had opted for my all time personal favourite, the deep-fried, golden, battered fresh haddock, with just a little vinegar and maybe a sprinkle of salt.

I could see that Tyrone was not eating his nuggets, just his chips, and that Honeysuckle was leaning over telling him that he must eat them up, and in doing so she had left her own wrapper and the haddock dangerously exposed on her lap. What a bit of luck!

Lionel was busy stuffing a cheeseburger the size of a dustbin lid into his mouth. As well as his usual nasty shorts and T shirt …I can barely begin to tell you this…he was wearing a back-to-front baseball cap with big splodges of fake seagull pooh all over it. And on the peak of the cap there was some writing. I flew a little lower so that I could read it for you.

It said, 'Damn Gulls!'

Talk about adding insult to injury. I was disgusted…but not surprised.

Lionel is one of those grown ups who concentrates hard when he is eating, as if nothing else were going on anywhere in the world. Lionel doesn't have meals, he has feeding time, like animals have in a zoo. Lionel never says that he has eaten enough or had sufficient, Lionel says that he's fit to bursting or that he's had a good gut's full, and that's why his belly is so big and fat and purple.

Lionel opened his mouth, and what a monstrous mouth it was, with a collection of teeth so haphazard that you might think they were gathered together from a box of leftovers at the natural history museum; a couple of walrus tusks, some chomping teeth from a sad old crocodile with gum disease, and a few yellowy brown horse's teeth from the knacker's yard chucked in for good measure.

Me in the Natural History Museum... so this is where Lionel got his teeth!

He crammed the burger in and the jaws and terrible teeth began to get to work mercilessly together, and the helpless cheeseburger had no chance.

Suddenly, Lionel stopped chewing, and a look of disgust came over his face.

'Uuugh!' He spluttered, spitting out bits of cheese and bread and burger all over Honeysuckle's nice flowery dress. 'They're trying to poison me…'

Lionel reached into his mouth and pulled out a half chewed baby lettuce leaf.

'Disgustin' filth! Where's it say on the box 'May contain salad', eh? I'll sue 'em, that's what I'll do,' he said, before adding. 'I'll just finish the burger first though.'

I circled on to a lower flight path, some ten feet above the heads of the Trumpers. They couldn't see me, because they were still too busy eating.

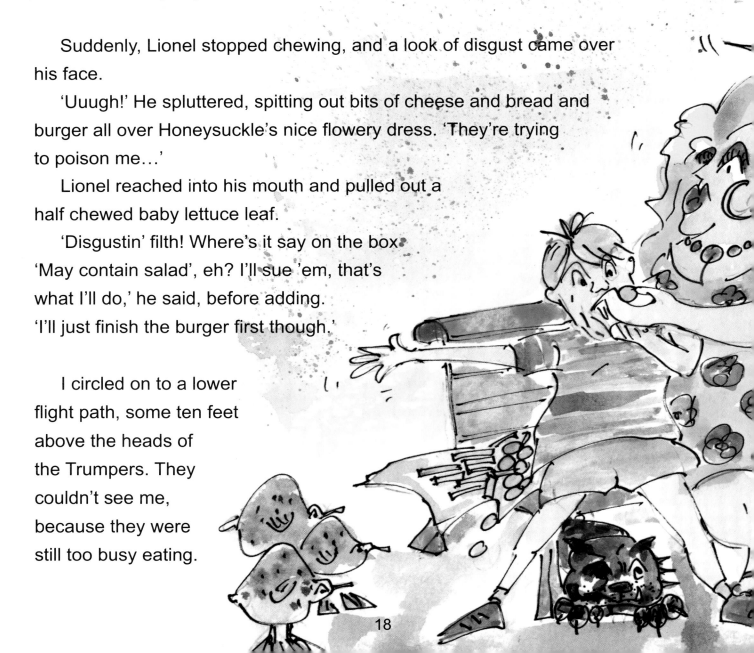

Listening carefully, I could hear a strange noise, rather like a belching hippopotamus suffering from a severe case of hiccups and indigestion and wind.

It was Lionel eating. All in all, I decided that it would be far too dangerous to try and steal a burger from anywhere near such a terrifying and dangerous place as his mouth.

Honeysuckle had become very cross with Tyrone and was trying to prise his jaws apart with her fingers.

'You got to eat 'em, Tyrone! They're good for you…' she said.

'I only wants them chips, our ma…' said Tyrone, through gritted teeth.

'They're expensive… that's why they're called nuggets!'

'They're cold and dry and hard and I hates 'em…'

'There's kiddies starving all over the world…' said Honeysuckle.

'Send 'em to them then. I'll pay the postage with me pocket money…' said Tyrone.

'You ain't getting no pocket money!!'

'Well, how am I supposed to send 'em then, stupid?'

Honeysuckle grabbed Tyrone by the nostrils, sealing them off and stopping his breathing and he had to open his mouth to gasp for air. She popped a nugget in and Tyrone screamed and spat it out.

The nugget hit Sabre who yelped and whimpered because it was so hard and because he was such a wus. The dog turned to see that Tyrone

The great chicken nugget chase

had dropped the entire wrapper. The other nuggets were now rolling away and gathering pace down the street and were being chased by the posse of fluffy, squeaky seagull chicks who had been hanging out by the bins, skittering and scuttling with the daft dog snapping at their backsides and, as if by magic, all the gulls of the village who suddenly came squawking down out of nowhere in hot pursuit to pinch the nuggets from the grasping beaks of the fat chicks…

Such mayhem, it really was delicious to see the Trumpers in such a state of panic and confusion, and I could see that I was going to get that piece of haddock!

That fish of my wildest dreams.

For my princess.

The Flight Log

These are my flight log extracts for the next few seconds…

Flight Log 12.6.2005
Subject - haddock
attack
Enemy - the Trumpers
Target - deep fry -
golden haddock -
mission - snatch
haddock and
splattt Lionel -

25 feet
Fast approach
from rear -
losing what
altitude
I have
left.

20 feet
Situation
unchanged

25 feet from target

Fast approach from rear. Losing altitude. Situation unchanged. Lionel troughing out. Honeysuckle ranting. Tyrone picking up chips from tarmac and eating them.

20 feet and closing

Haddock still exposed.

15 feet

Consider aborting mission.

Lionel stopped eating. Lionel looking around.

Reaches for orange Tango.

Hear noise like baboon having bottom boiled in a tea urn.

It is Lionel swilling the Tango.

10 feet

Momentarily lose sight of prize haddock.

Close up Lionel's disgusting baseball cap with cheap and unkind slogan and fake embossed seagull pooh.

Snap decision taken. Decide this is to be a joint mission.

Snatch haddock *and* punish Lionel …

5 feet

Too late to abort.

One flap veer 45 degrees starboard, exposing vulnerable undercarriage to back of Lionel's stupid head and peak of his wrong way round baseball cap.

splattt Lionel all over cap and back of silly Fat Willy Tshirt.

And I mean *all* over.

Lionel jumps up and roars in anger 'Noooo…!'

As if in slow motion, the can of tango spins up into the air and then clatters onto the street and rolls away. Sabre, having had no success with the nuggets, waddles over and stops the can with his nose and laps up the fizzing orange liquid. The bubbles make him sneeze and show his teeth like he is smiling, which of course dogs can't really do because they're too silly.

Lionel's beloved mega, giant, cheesy, dustbin-lid sized burger also flies up into the air like a half-eaten flying saucer, and then crash lands on the street in front of him. Inconsolable with grief, Lionel lurches forward onto the ground on his pudgy hands and knees and begins to scoop everything, and I mean everything, into a filthy, revolting heap; burger, greasy wrappers, gravel, lettuce leaf, baseball hat, chips, cigarette ends and all.

Ground Zero

In a nano second, I am at the fresh fried battered haddock; it is better than I ever dared imagine. This is a piece of haddock of which dreams are made, and I would swear if I did not know better that it is glistening like pure gold. Untouched. Fit for a princess. *The* princess.

The Haddock...glistening like pure gold

I dip my head and open my beak and with a loud and triumphant squawk I snatch the fish from her lap and with three hard wing beats I fly up and up and up and away. A successful getaway! Phew!

You know what? I'm good. Very good.

So good in fact that, call me a showman if you will, I could think of nothing better than a low level Gully fly past with full splattts. and so out of sight of the Trumpers I flew behind a building and turned and again made the fast approach, and this time with the fresh fried, battered, still glowing haddock held firmly in my beak, majestically I buzzed the unpleasant baseball cap and cluster bombed the Trumpers with a magnificent series of splattts. and then with a disco boogie woogie wiggle of my tail feathers, a double spin and a loop the loop and a whoopee-doo! I flew off and away.

Only once I'd reached a safe height did I wheel above and take a good look at the carnage below; Tyrone snivelling, Sabre whimpering and whining in fear as the posse of young gulls returned looking for more food and revenge, while Lionel, yes Lionel, was left groveling on his knees and sobbing and swearing and eating fag ends and dirt and gravel, totally polka-dotted and splatttered by yours truly!

Honeysuckle was sitting bemused and open-mouthed on the bench, staring at her empty fish and chip wrapper.

Whoopee-doo!

'Oi!' said Lionel. 'What about a song now then, eh?'

'*Oh, I do like to be beside the seaside…*' croaked Honeysuckle.

Somehow, I may be wrong, but at that very moment I don't think Honeysuckle did particularly like being beside the seaside.

I spent some time above, allowing the fresh fried battered haddock to cool sufficiently for the princess; god forbid her little beak get scalded. I looked down admiringly on my work and, isn't it funny how things work out sometimes, I could see something on the street, a shape formed from my cluster bomb splattt that was just like a crab. A seagull splattt crab that I had created. All on my own. Me. An artist. My goodness, I thought, I'm going to become an artist, a Cornish artist, a famous Cornish artist. Why not? There's plenty of others who do. I flew back to the gullery to give the princess her haddock and tell her the exciting news.

The End

Lionel grovelling...
oh, and my marvellous splattt crab!

Also available

Three mischievous adventures of the wicked seagull on CD

The range of Gully story books

...so save it all for me!

and pickles. fish fingers and scampi too. vinegar. mushy pea's (yuck!). beans. jumbo hot dog. onion rings. gherkins and pizza and dad's sauce...

The Author

The creator, author and illustrator of Gully, Jon Cleave, lives in the heart of the lovely old Cornish fishing village of Port Isaac with his wife Caroline and boys Jakes, George and Theo.... oh yes, and hundreds and hundreds of squealing, squawking, screaming seagulls!